AS IF... AS IF...

First Published 2018
Printed in China by Toppan Leefung Printing (Shanghai) Co., Ltd.
No. 106 Qingda Road, Pudong, New Area, Shanghai, 201201, China

Thank you to Courtney Chow, Yingniao Dai and Marlo Garnsworthy (in alphabetical order) who were involved in translating and editing this book.

Our thanks also go out to Elyse Williams for her creative efforts in preparing this edition for publication.

As If... As If...

Written by Wenjun QIN
Illustrated by Xun LIU

A little girl with little red shoes strolls into the garden after the rain. It is as if she has been captivated by an enchanting fairy tale.

With the help of her rich imagination, she feels as if she can read the mind of each creature around her.

Look! An earthworm burrows out of a small mound of soil and promptly wriggles back, as if praying: "Don't get me wet, pleaaase! I've just dressed up!"

A puppy rolls around on the lush lawn and immediately hurries away, as if realizing: "How could I tread on this lovely, green velvet carpet?"

Tiny petals from the pear tree flies off, as if they were elegant butterflies. The spring rain has moistened the lawn in the garden. Mist is rising from dewy grass, as if it were a chiffon veil being lifted.

The sun appears in the sky, slowly, leisurely, and a little drowsily, as if yawning, "So many creatures are waiting for me..." At that thought, the sun wakes up and beams brightly.

A battalion of ants whispers at the puddle's edge, as if complaining, "How could they forget to build a bridge over this large lake?" A timely petal drifts toward them, which they quickly and contentedly climb onto.

The pink peach blossoms are especially well-dressed, as if waiting. "No one has come to compliment me yet..."

A kitten wakes up, arching and yawning at the dripping spring garden. It is as if she is murmuring, "I wonder which are thinner - raindrops or my whiskers?"

A plump, white mushroom crouches amid the waving grass. He does not feel like moving at all.

Drops of rain hang from branches, as if they are cold crystal icicles. One drop drips down and taps a snail on her shell. The snail, hiding in her cozy home, starts to panic, as if worrying, "Is that a guest knocking at my door? I haven't even washed my face yet!"

A scarab beetle comes and goes, as if he is running late. "Oops! This isn't where I need to be!"

A dragonfly rests on the little girl's finger, as if he is an emerald ring with a pair of silver wings.

A peacock is jabbering loudly in the distance. He is ready to fan out his feathers, as if announcing, "I need to dry my new jacket after the rain!"

A white swan gazes at the snow-white clouds, as if pondering, "Have the black swans whitened up after being washed in the spring shower?"

A black swan is also staring at the fluffy clouds, as if longing, "If only I could rest on the soft clouds for a whole night!"

A lively lark has become interested in calligraphy. He glides around and writes words in the air. He keeps cheeping, as if explaining, "I'm happy as long as my writing is legible!"

A spider crawls out and weaves her web hastily, as if she has made up her mind. "I'll make the biggest web of all!"

A leaf, blown off a willow, swirls in the wind, as if dancing and singing, "I used to hate heights. I feel much better closer to the ground."

A three-hundred-year-old tortoise is rubbing a pile of pebbles, as if sighing, "This one feels like the shell of my eldest brother and that one the shell of my second eldest brother!" The garden after the rain has flooded him with memories.

A red ladybug takes a break on a wild berry. She tightly embraces the berry with her thread-like arms, as if declaring, "This is as red and as pretty as me!"

A bunny hops onto the lawn. She gawks at the wet green leaves on the ground, as if hesitating. "Will I turn green if I roll here?"

A little squirrel sees the little girl and nudges her, as if asking, "Do you have chewing gum? My hut is leaking, so I want to patch the hole."

Every blade of grass is having a sweet dream. The smallest blade bends down, as if praying, "It has taken me so much time and energy to grow to this height. Pleaaase don't trample me!"

A little hedgehog looks ashamed, as if blaming himself. Did his spikes make those holes in the sky, letting the rain fall through? He curls into a spiny ball, as if comforting myself, "At least, I can hide my white belly now!"

Behind the hedgehog, a little raccoon is waiting quietly, as if she wants to borrow a spike from him to skewer wild berries. She has a lot of patience. "Not all stars twinkle simultaneously at dusk. I'm the shy one that waits until it's completely dark."

In the most tranquil corner of the garden is a dry tree hollow. The little girl sits down in the hollow and relaxes in the warmth and aroma, as if she can hear flowers blooming.

The butterfly dances, as if counting the flowers. A little bird folds her wings, as if she were a touch-me-not plant folding her leaves.

The little girl looks around in joy...
This garden is spectacular!

She hears dandelions swaying, as if requesting, "Give me a smile!"

So, she closes her eyes and smiles, as she feels a slight tickle. A hairy little thing is rubbing her little arm,

as if it is the squirrel's tail...

as if it is the bunny's ear...

as if it is the swan's wing...

as if it is the puppy's head...

as if... as if...

The little girl sways her arms gently, as if she were a blade of grass, and laughs happily, as if she were a blooming flower.

She is as happy and as beautiful as the garden after the rain.

I write as if I find beauty and peace of mind

By Wenjun Qin

I love reading and writing to complement the many peaceful elements in my personality. I especially enjoy writing articles and short stories in calm moments, as if words and sentences could then flow freely from my soul, my consciousness, and my fantasies, instead of being squeezed out or over-carefully crafted. *As If... As If...* was born in a very tranquil, ethereal, relaxed state of mind.

In the spring of 2013, my husband and I rented a small, quiet apartment near Central Park in New York and lived there for a month. Yingniao, my daughter and translator of this book, was then studying at Columbia University. We waited happily every day for her to join us for dinner.

While I was having a family vacation in New York, I listened to flowers blooming. I watched butterflies dancing leisurely. I spent more time with my family. Oh, that simple, light, evanescent spring!

On a rainy morning, I was sitting in my apartment, listening to the rain tapping on the window. A little pigeon, wet-through, took shelter from the rain under the eave. Sentimental coos came out of her little throat, as if she had sighed. I was affected somehow, like a child. In the afternoon, the sky cleared up. I took a stroll alone in Central Park. I walked through the thick woods. I stared at the sky covered with clouds. I tiptoed along the path under layers of petals. I breathed in the refreshing air... I had walked a long way when I caught a glimpse of a young mother and her toddler girl with little red shoes on.

The memory of that spring in Central Park lingers on, as if it faded and then freshened up again. The precious tranquility in the world never fails to move me to tears.

At the dinner table, I shared my wonderful experience with Yingniao, who has always understood me so well. A little squirrel once tickled her arm, begging for snacks. So many lovable little creatures, such as puppies, kittens, and birdies she encountered and felt like they were "talking" to her. I drew inspiration from her interesting encounters with animals.

I have cherished one book from the first edition of *As If... As If...* I want to pass the story on to my grandchildren one day and watch them indulge in the prose and mood of beauty and peace. Music, arts, and literature are the wings that help souls fly. I believe that readers who love beautiful and elegant literature from childhood are more likely to make ethical decisions and live bright, happy lives.

I would like to thank Liu Xun, my illustrator, and Yingniao, my daughter and translator, for their lovely contributions. Looking through the window, I have the feeling that it is going to rain again. I will continue writing, with beauty and peace of mind, which makes me feel proud and lucky.

The Author

Wenjun Qin was born in Shanghai, China, in 1954. She is a famous Chinese children's book writer, having won over 50 awards in China and abroad. In 2009, she became the first Chinese writer to be shortlisted for the Astrid Lindgren Memorial Award. She was nominated for the 2002 Hans Christian Andersen Award. She has published 58 children's books and written more than 6 million words. To her, being a children's book author is the world's best job. She has a great understanding of what her readers like.

After the Rain

By Xun Liu

When I was an art student, I often went sketching outdoors after the rain. I loved drawing amid moist air, dark tree bark, glittering leaves, and fragrant grass. When I read *As If... As If...*, what caught my eye first were the words "after the rain." I remember what Ms. Qin wrote: "The spring rain has moistened the lawn in the garden. Mist is rising from dewy grass, as if it were a chiffon veil being lifted." Yes, mist after the rain always spreads like a chiffon veil!

On an early morning in April, after the rain, I rode my bicycle alone to the countryside, hoping to gather inspiration from nature. The storm lasted through the night and bent down the branches of the trees along the path. A few wild ducks were swimming silently in the misty pond far away. Petals from peach trees and pear trees were lying everywhere on the ground. Clear puddles mirrored daisies. The early morning after a stormy night was simply serene but amazing. Every few steps, I was happily taken by surprise. Every time I turned around, I could see something almost overpoweringly beautiful.

I very much enjoyed illustrating *As If... As If...* Finally, I was able to express, in a picture book, my deep fondness of nature after the rain.

The Illustrator

Xun Liu resides in Nanjing, China. She studied craft design at university and has worked as a designer and animator. Due to her great interest in oil painting, after working for many years, she found herself back studying at the China Central Academy of Fine Art. There she studied classical painting techniques. She began creating children's picture books after her daughter was born. In 2015, Tooth, Tooth, Onto the Roof! won the Feng Zikai Chinese Children's Picture Book Award. Now, she draws every day, while teaching drawing on the weekends and sharing all she has learned with lovely children.